# ALL NIGHT, ALL DAY:

*A Child's First Book*
*of African-American Spirituals*

# ALL NIGHT, ALL DAY:

*A Child's First Book
of African-American Spirituals*

selected and illustrated by
## ASHLEY BRYAN
musical arrangements by
## DAVID MANNING THOMAS

Aladdin Paperbacks
New York  London  Toronto  Sydney  Singapore

*To the memory of*
*Arthur Duplex Wright III,*
*World War II comrade, scholar, and*
*dear friend:*
*"Angels Watching Over Thee"*
*—A. B.*

*To my wife, Gale; to our new child, Leandria;*
*and to the principal of Caledonia Elementary School,*
*Mrs. Stella Loeb-Munson*
*—D. M. T.*

First Aladdin Paperbacks edition January 2004

Copyright © 1991 by Ashley Bryan

ALADDIN PAPERBACKS
An imprint of Simon & Schuster
Children's Publishing Division
1230 Avenue of the Americas
New York, NY 10020

Also available in Atheneum Books for Young Readers hardcover edition.

Manufactured in China
6  8  10  9  7  5
0817 SCP
The Library of Congress has cataloged the hardcover edition as follows:
All night, all day: a child's first book of African-American spirituals / selected and illustrated by
Ashley Bryan.
1 score.
For voice and piano.
Includes chord symbols.
Summary: A selection of twenty spirituals, that distinctive music from the time of slavery.
Includes piano accompaniment and guitar chords.
ISBN 0-689-31662-3 (hc.)
1. Spirituals (Songs)—Juvenile. [1. Spirituals (Songs)]
I. Bryan, Ashley.
M1670.A4 1991
90-753145
ISBN 978-0-689-86786-6 (Aladdin pbk.)

# CONTENTS

# All Night, All Day

**Medium to fast tempo**

Arr. David M. Thomas

# Chatter with the Angels

Arr. David M. Thomas

Chat-ter with the an-gels, soon in the mor-nin', Chat-ter with the an-gels, in that land!

Chat-ter with the an-gels, soon in the mor-nin', Chat-ter with the an-gels, join that band!

I hope to join that band and Chat-ter with the an-gels all day long!

I hope to join that band and Chat-ter with the an-gels all day long!

9

# Who's That a-Comin' Over Yonder

Arr. David M. Thomas

# Somebody's Knocking at Your Door

Arr. David M. Thomas

# This Little Light of Mine

Arr. David M. Thomas

# Behold That Star

Arr. David M. Thomas

# I'm a-Going to Eat at the Welcome Table

**Heavy gospel feel, medium tempo**

Arr. David M. Thomas

I'm a-going to eat at the wel-come ta - - ble,
I'm a-going to feast on milk and ho - - ney,

I'm a-going to eat at the wel-come ta - ble, some of these days.
I'm a-going to feast on milk and ho - ney, some of these days.

I'm a-going to eat at the wel-come ta - - ble, I'm going to
I'm a-going to feast on milk and ho - - ney, I'm going to

eat at the wel-come ta - ble, some of these days.
feast on milk and ho - ney, some of these days.

# O When the Saints Go Marching In

Arr. David M. Thomas

# I Stood on the River of Jordan

Arr. David M. Thomas

With much emotion (♩ = 92)

1. I stood on the ri - ver of Jor - dan, To see the ships come sail - ing o - ver,
2. O sis - ter, you bet - ter be read - y,
3. O bro - ther, you bet - ter be read - y,

Stood on the ri - ver of Jor - dan, To see the ships sail by.
Sis - ter, you bet - ter be read - y,
Bro - ther, you bet - ter be read - y,

*Refrain*

O mourn - er, don't you weep! When you see the ships come sail - ing o - ver,

O mourn - er, don't you weep! When you see the ships sail by.

# Get on Board

Arr. David M. Thomas

# Peter, Go Ring the Bells

Arr. David M. Thomas

# He's Got the Whole World in His Hands

Arr. David M. Thomas

# Wade in the Water

Arr. David M. Thomas

# There's No Hiding Place

arr. David M. Thomas

# The Rocks and the Mountains

**With rhythmic energy** ( ♩ = about 96 )

Arr. David M. Thomas

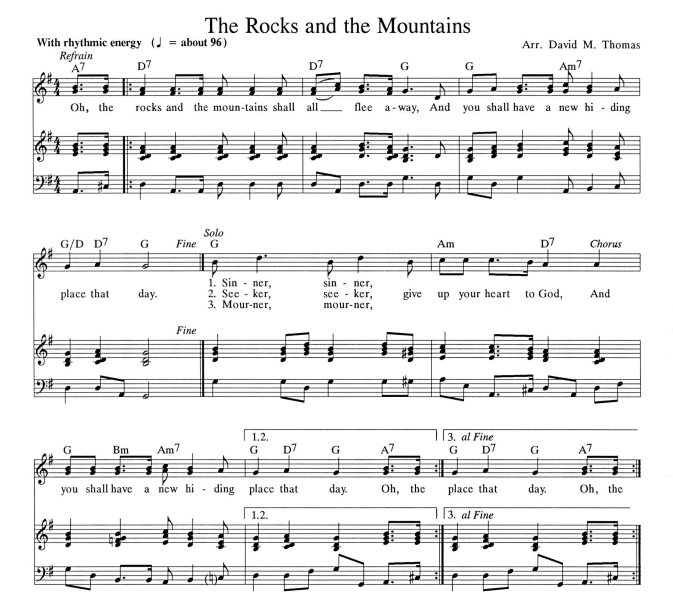

# I'm Gonna Sing

Arr. David M. Thomas

# Open the Window, Noah

Arr. David M. Thomas

# O Won't You Sit Down

# Now Let Me Fly

Arr. David M. Thomas

# Great Big Stars

Arr. David M. Thomas

1. O my lit - tle soul's gon - na shine, shine! O my lit - tle soul's gon - na shine, shine!
2. All a - round the world gon - na shine, shine! All a - round the world gon - na shine, shine!

# A NOTE ON THE SPIRITUALS

I have subtitled this collection "A Child's First Book of African-American Spirituals." It could really be called "Spirituals for the Young and ALL!"

Wherever I travel, people sing these songs. Often they do not know that they are singing spirituals. They associate the melodies with their churches, schools, camps, or clubs, and are surprised when told that they are singing spirituals. It is a tribute to the artistry of these songs that they are loved and sung, but it would also be good to know something of the origin of these beautiful songs.

The songs called spirituals come to us from the time of slavery in the United States. Their creation ends with the abolition of slavery. The names of the individual creators of these songs have been lost, but we know that they come from the musical genius of African-American slaves.

Almost a thousand of these songs have been collected since the end of the Civil War. They are unique in the song literature of the world and are considered America's most distinctive contribution to world music.

I have been compiling books devoted solely to selections of these songs because there were no collections of them for young people. I hope that as the singers grow with these books of spirituals, they will later give us books of their own selections from this great body of song. The spirituals will then appear with the regularity and diversity of presentation that they deserve.

My musician friend David Manning Thomas has set rhythmic and harmonic piano accompaniments in support of the melodies of the spirituals, which give something of the subtle swing and tonal color that characterize these songs.

The guitar chords are indicated as well. Occasionally, an adjustment of guitar chords to harmonize with the piano accompaniment may be necessary.

Verses for each spiritual are noted. You may know other verses or even wish to add verses of your own as you go along. Sing them, too! Variation and invention are at the heart of the spiritual.

David Manning Thomas and I hope that this presentation will extend the singing repertory of the African-American spiritual and will bring vocal and visual pleasure to its audience.

Ashley Bryan
Islesford, Maine 1990